Jacob Thomas Elwell, Charles Henry Pope

The Elwell Family in America

A Genealogy of Robert Elwell of Dorchester and Gloucester

Jacob Thomas Elwell, Charles Henry Pope

The Elwell Family in America
A Genealogy of Robert Elwell of Dorchester and Gloucester

ISBN/EAN: 9783337307493

Printed in Europe, USA, Canada, Australia, Japan

Cover: Foto ©Raphael Reischuk / pixelio.de

More available books at **www.hansebooks.com**

THE
ELWELL FAMILY IN AMERICA:

A Genealogy

OF

ROBERT ELWELL,

OF DORCHESTER AND GLOUCESTER, MASS.,

AND THE GREATER PART OF HIS DESCENDANTS TO THE
FIFTH GENERATION.

WITH A LIST OF

*Revolutionary Soldiers of the name who enlisted
from the State of Massachusetts.*

COMPILED BY THE LATE
REV. JACOB THOMAS ELWELL (1844—1888).

REVISED BY
REV. CHARLES HENRY POPE,

Member of the N. E. Historic Genealogical Society, compiler of The Dorchester Pope Family;
The Cheney Genealogy; The Gospels Combined; The Records of the
First Church, Dorchester, 1636—1734; etc.

BOSTON, MASS.:
PUBLISHED BY CHARLES H. POPE,
221 Columbus Avenue.
1899.

THE ELWELL FAMILY IN AMERICA:

Robert Elwell of Dorchester, Mass., 1634, and some of His Descendants.

Robert Elwell is known to have been a resident of Dorchester, in the Colony of Massachusetts Bay (now a part of the city of Boston) in the year 1634. No documentary evidence has come to light to show his family connections, social estate or occupation. In the Dorchester Town Records for Sept. 1, 1634, we read: "It is ordered that the Lott which was granted formerly to John Rocket shall be transferred to Robert Elway" [Elwell].

On a map of certain lots in town, printed in the book of Records, we may see Lt No. 49 marked for J. Rocket; and No. 74, 3 acres, marked R. Elwell.

Jan. 2, 1637. "It is ordered that Mr. Holland and Robert Elwell shall have that slip of upland and marsh lyeing from the further Corner of Mr. Richards lott to their houses leaving a free passige for carts, or any other Carriadges that way."

"It is ordered that Mr. Holland have all the rest of the marsh to the pyne necke after 4 akers granuted to Good: Greenway and one aker more to be reserved to the disposall of the Plantation. Mr. Glover and Good: Gaylor to lay it out."

"It is ordered that Robert Elwell shall have two acres of marsh at Mr. Ludlow necke."

"It is ordered that Robert Elwell, Bray Wilkeins, Henery Way, James Priest, shall have allotments at Mannings Moone."

"March 18th   It is ordered that all the hoame lotts and great lotts shall be sufficiently fenced against swine and great cattle p' the 25 of this month, on payne of thre shillings for every goad found defective, to be levied p' distresse, besides damedges."

In the lists of allotments at the Neck and Cows Pasture we find Robert Elwell's to be: In the Neck. 2 akers, 2 qurs. 39 rodes. In the rest of the division of the land: 2 akers, 2 qurs. 39 rodes. The 3d of April, 1638, "It is ordered that the allotment which was formerly granuted on Mannings Moon shall be 8 akers to James Priest the rest to Robert Elwell in pt'e of his great lott."

June 8, 1640. "John Holland hath sold unto Mr. Mather all his Commons at the great neck which is eight akers 3 qutrs 79 Rodes beeing his owne p'portion of right there, and also Robert Elwells which he purchased."

These are all the allusions to Robert Elwell found in the Records; he may have been mentioned in the earlier pages, long ago lost from the book, in which were recorded the land grants and acts of the proprietors before 1632.

The last record may refer to a sale made at the time of his removal from town.

In the Records of The Colony we find the following references to Robert Elwell :

"1635. Aug. 4th. Att the Court holden att Newtowne [Cambridge] John Holland, being att the Eastward, affirmeth that Mr. Thomas Wonnarton threatned to sinke his boate if he would not pay him a debt that Henry Way ought him, & called him roage & Knave, & said they were all soe in the Bay, & that hee hoped to see all their throates cutt, & that hee could find in his heart to begin with him, & thereupon strucke him upon the head ; and when the said Holland tould him, if Way ought him any money hee might recover it by lawe, to weh Wonnarton answered that they had noe lawe for them but to sterve them ; the like Bray Wilkinson & Robert Ellwell witnesseth against Wonarton ; whereupon it was ordered that the said Wonarton should putt in sufficient suryties for his good behavr, & in the mean tyme to remaine in durance."

"1636/7. March 7. A capias was grannted to John Stretton to bring Kibbe & Elwell before the Governor."

1640, May 13. "Psons made free the 13th of the 8th mo. 1640." Among the 144 persons who then became freemen of the Colony, or citizens in the fullest sense, capable of voting at General elections and being eligible for election to the General Court, etc., stands the name of Robert Elwell. In order to become a Freemen of the Colony one must, at that day, be a member of one of the churches in the Colony, and be recommended by his minister or some other man of standing as a man of good character and loyalty ; and an oath was administered to each man on his entering the honorable list, pledging him to fidelity and service to the government of the Colony.

His name may be found in one more record of the Massachusetts Court : "1647. At a session of ye Courte of Eleccon, begunne the last 4th day of ye 8 month, 1647.

In ans'r. to ye peticon of Robert Elwell, Wm. Browne, & Mr. Dudbridge, a review was grannted of an accou between them & Mr. Tuttle, at ye next Court of Assistants, so as they give him fowerteene dayes notice thereof."

Not far from the time when he became a freeman of the Colony Robert Elwell removed from Dorchester to Salem, as is seen in town records.

He appears as an owner of land in Gloucester in the second month (April) 1642, when he bought of Mr. Milward "two acres of upland lying in the harbor, between the lots of John Collins and Zebulon Hill, and running from his house northerly over the next swamp." This lot was situated, as Babson believes, a little east of what is now Centre street. In 1651 he had a grant of "Stage Neck," now called Rock Neck. His will specifies the location of other lands he owned. He was counted a citizen of Salem till he actually resided at Gloucester. Children were there baptized until the close of 1641, and his name is on the list of members of the church in 1642. Not far from 1649 [in the opinion of Perley Derby] he made his home in Gloucester ; and in that year was chosen one of the selectmen. The General Court appointed him one of the two "commissioners to end small causes" in Gloucester, in 1651, and he did considerable business in this judicial position. He was a member of the committee to erect a new meeting-house in 1661. We are fortunate in possessing

The Will of Robert Elwell, the Immigrant.

I Robert Elwell of Gloucester in the County of Essex in New England being by God's providence cast upon my Bed of sicknesse & weaknesse & not knowing how near the time of my departure out of this world may be & withal knowing it to be the mind & will of God that a man should Set his house in order before he dye do therefore in order to the disposing of my estate & Goods make knowne & declare this my last Will and Testament in manner & fforme following. Imprimis I give & bequeath unto my eldest Sonne Samuel Elwell the House I now dwell in together with all the Barnes & buildings neare adjoyneing which are same and not otherwise hereafter disposed off, as also all the Neck of Land whereupon my said House standeth except what is hereafter disposed of to my sonne Thomas and all the rest of my Land & Meadow both here & at the Eastern Poynt and little good Harbour & elsewhere except only what is hereafter bequeathed to my sonnes John and Thomas otherwise except what is hereafter excepted I give all my Sayd Housing & Lands above expressed to him my sayd sonne Samuel and his Heires forever provided always & it is my will & meaning that my sayd sonne Samuel shall maintaine myself & his mother my wife during the terme of our Natural lives with convenient & sufficient mayntenance both for clothing & dyet & washing (it always being understood that our bedding & household we doe not dispose but make use of it for our selves whilst we live as we see meet) but otherwise he shall provide us & find both his mother and myselfe with the above-sayd necessaryes of food & Rayment during our Natural Lives sufficiently & also wood for firing convenient & all other necessarys & attendance both in sicknesse & health & so to enter upon the improvement of my sayd Living when I shall appoynt him in case I live & in case I now dye to enter upon the sayd Living presently after my decease. Also I do hereby give & bequeath unto my sayd sonne all my carts ploughs & tackling belonging unto them & all my other Tools for carrying on the worke abovesayd. Item I give and bequeath unto my sonne John Elwell three Acres of my meadow at little good Harbour to him and his Heirs forever. Item I give unto my sonne Isaac Elwell my cloake after my decease. Item I give & bequeath unto my sonne Joseph a yeareling steer after my decease. Item I give & bequeath unto my sonne Thomas Elwell the Half acre of Land with the orchyard his House standeth upon and one Acre of meadow or Marsh at Starke naught Harbour (so commonly called) and also one yeareling after my decease to injoy the abovesayd to him his Heirs Execrs. Admins. or Assignes for ever. Item I give & bequeath unto my Daughter Deliber* a Two yeare old Heifer after my decease. Item I give & bequeath unto Samuel Elwell my grandsonne all that my house & Land his Father now liveth in & upon lying & being Situate on the other side of the River or Harbour in Glocester aforesayd fower Acres of said Land being in and adjoining neare sayd House & two Acres being meadow and lying by the Lott to him & his Heires for ever & in case the sayd Samuel my Grand Sonne doe dye without Heires it shall then fall to my next eldest Grandsonne & so in the like Case of Mortality from one to another of my Grandsonnes. And this my sayd Grand Son Samuel to have after my decease and to pay twenty shillings unto his grandmother my wife. Item I give & bequeath unto my Grand Sonne Robert Elwell who now lives with me all my quarter part of my Katch in case he abides with his father and help him. And the sayd Robert shall pay unto his sayd Grandmother my wife the full summ of foure pounds after my decease. Item I give & bequeath all my wearing Apparell to my Sonnes to be divided equally amongst them after my decease. Item I give & bequeath all my household stuffe or Goodes such as Bedding pots pewter Brasse stooles & Chayres or Chests & Boxes unto all my Children to be equally divided amongst them after my decease & the decease of my wife. And whereas it is above expressed that my sonne Samuel shall have my House I now dwell in after my decease my will & meaning is so long only as my wife aforesayd & hee my sayd sonne do agree & like to live together. But if there be any disagreement betweene them & that his sayd mother like wrather to live by her selfe, I doe hereby declare it to be my mind & will fully that then my sayd son shall depart the House & leave it to his mother & shee shall injoy it to her owne peculiar use & behoof during her Naturall Life he still providing for her in all Respects as abovesayd during her terme of Life. Also whereas it is above expressed that my sonne Samuel shall have this my living abovesayd to him & his Heirs forever my will & meaning is & I do hereby appoynt my Grand-sonne Robert (son of sayd Samuel) that now liveth with me to be the next Immediate Heir unto this my Sayd Living after his father my sayd son Samuel to injoy the

* Dolliver.

same to him & his Heires for ever and in case the sayd Robert doe die without Heire it shal then fall to the next eldest of my Grandsonnes surviving & so in like case of mortality from one to another to the next eldest of my Grandsonnes surviving. Item I give unto my Grand sonne William Elwell (sonne to my sonne Josiah deceased) a calfe of this yeares breeding. Item I give & bequeath unto my deare & loving wife two Milch Cowes for her owne peculiar use & to dispose of as shee shall see meet & doe also order my son Samuel to provide & bring home ffodder for them during the term of her natural Life & in case he does not provide for them as above sayd it shall be in the power of my Executors to take away one acre of the meadow at the eastern poynt for the purpose above sayd. Item I give & bequeath unto my wife the use & benefit of of the Garden by my now dwelling House to have & improve as she shall see meet during the terme of her natural Life. And all the rest of my Cattell not here disposed off both Cowes & oxen & other younger Cattell I give unto my Sonne Samuel Elwell except only what may be for the discharging of my debts & charges of my executors concerning the ordering of my estate in disposing & distributing & other necessary expenses that they may be at one way or another about the same. Also I leave all my houshold Goodes with my wife for her use during her Naturall Life & after her decease to be distributed as above sayd. And that this my last Will and Testament may be truly performed I doe intreat my deare & well beloved Friend Mr John Emerson & Jeffrey Parsons Sen. to be the Executors of this my last will & Testament & doe hereby constitute ordayne authorize & impower them in all Respects the sayd Executors to see it fully executed as performed.

And furthermore I doe give two ewe sheep to my wife & the rest of them to my sonne Samuel. Also I doe give my Horse to my wife to have the use of it during her natural Life & my sonne Samuel to provide him winter meat. And my Colt I give unto my sonne Samuel. And in case my sonne Samuel doe not provide Comfortably for his sayd mother my wife according to what is above expressed I doe hereby Authorize & impower my sayd executors to take away & to order & dispose of the sayd Living & Cattell given to my sonne to any whom they shall see meet for my wife's Comfortable subsistence as abovesayd during her Naturall Life. And for the full Confirmation of this my last Will and Testament I have hereunto set my Hand & Seale the fiveteenth day of this Instant May Anno. Dom. one thousand six hundred & eighty three.

Sealed & Subscribed
in the p'sence of us   [SEAL.]
The marke of O John Row Sen.   The marke of ꝛ ROBERT ELWELL.
Ruth Emerson Jun.

John Row & Ruth Emerson made oath in Court at Salem the 26 of June 1683: that they were present & did see the said Robert Elwell signe seale & declare the above written to be his last will & testament. & that he was then to their best understanding of good understanding & that they signed as witnesses to the above written.   Attest HILLIARD VEREN Cler.

The inventory brings out no points of special interest.

The will of Alce, widow of Robert Elwell, dated March 21, 1690-1, bequeathed her estate to her five daughters, to be equally divided between them, except that Alce Bennett should have a small Iron Kettle. The inventory mentions the two cows and two sheep mentioned in her husband's will, and some money due her from Samuel Elwell, with a few other items; and refers to an agreement made with her two sons, Samuel and Robert Leach. Admin. June 30, 1691.

1. ROBERT[1] ELWELL, married first, ———. Joane ———; she died March 31, 1675. He married second, May 20, 1676, Alce, widow of ——— Leach, who survived him, and died April 10, 1691. He died May 18, 1683.

   Children:

   2.   i. SAMUEL,[2] b. in Dorchester about 1636.
        ii. "Second Child," bapt. at Salem, Aug. 28, 1639; d. æ. 6 mos.
   3. iii. JOHN,[2] bapt. at Salem, 23(11)1639-40.
   · 4. iv. ISAAC,[2] bapt. at Salem, 27(12)1641-2.

5.   v. Josiah.[2]
6.   vi. Joseph.[2]
    vii. Sara,[2] b. and d. in 1651.
    viii. Sarah,[2] b. May 12, 1652; d. Aug. 26, 1655.
7.   ix. Thomas,[2] b. Nov. 12, 1654.
    x. Jacob,[2] b. June 10, 1657; d. May 21, 1658.
    xi. Richard,[2] bapt. April 11, 1658.
    xii. Mary,[2] m. Samuel Dolliver, of Gloucester. Children:
        1. *Samuel Dolliver,* b. July 3, 1658.
        2. *Mary Dolliver,* b. March 26, 1662.
        3. *Richard Dolliver,* b. April 18, 1665.
        4. *Sara Dolliver,* b. Dec. 29, 1667.
        5. *John Dolliver,* b. Sept. 2, 1671.

2. Samuel[2] Elwell (*Robert[1]*), born at Dorchester, in 1635 or 1636, married Esther, daughter of Osman or Osmund Dutch and Grace, his wife. He sold June 21, 1678, land given him by his father-in-law. Grace, widow of Osmund Dutch, sold to her son-in-law Samuel Elwell, Sen., a tract of salt marsh at Little Good Harbour, June 30, 1691. Alice Mecham, of Ipswich, widow; Grace Hodgskins, of Ipswich (who had sons, Thomas and Christopher, in 1701); and Mary, wife of Joseph Elwell, Samuel's brother, were also daughters of Mr. Dutch.

Samuel Elwell was one of the signers to the agreement with Rev. John Emerson about the town grist-mill, in May, 1661; and, in the year 1695, being then 60 years old, he deposed to the document.

He resided at Gloucester. He died about 1697. The widow died Sept. 6, 1721, aged about 82 years.

Children:

8.   i. Samuel,[3] b. March 14, 1659.
9.   ii. Jacob,[3] b. Aug. 10, 1662.
—10.   iii. Robert,[3] b. Dec. 13, 1664.
    iv. Esther,[3] b. Aug. 25, 1667.
    v. Sarah,[3] b. and d. in 1670.
11.   vi. Ebenezer,[3] b. Feb. 25, 1670–1.
    vii. Hannah,[3] b. Aug. 11, 1674; m. Jan. 2, 1695, Joseph Gardner.
    viii. Elizabeth,[3] b. July 30, 1678.
12.   ix. Thomas.[3] His house-lot in Gloucester is referred to in the description of the location of his brother Ebenezer's.

3. John[2] Elwell (*Robert[1]*), baptized at Salem, 23(11)1639–40, married Oct. 1, 1667, Jane Durin. He resided at Salem till about 1677; had grants of land in Gloucester, in 1677 and 1707. March 14, 1677, he sold land at the South Harbour in Salem to William Pinson, of Salem, fisherman, premises adjoining those of William Hollingworth, which he had bought Nov. 12, 1670, of John Clifford, rope-maker. He sold a tract of land at Long Beach to his son-in-law, John Smith, Jr., Feb. 6, 1702; and one at the Head of the Cape, June 12, 1707, to Richard Tarr. He was captured by the Indians, and died in captivity in February, 1710. Administration was granted to his only son, John, Jan. 19, 1712.

Children:

13.   i. John,[3] b. Oct. 14, 1668.
    ii. Jane,[3] b. Nov. 23, 1671.
    iii. Susanna,[3] b. at Gloucester, April 24, 1678.
    iv. Mary,[3] b. Feb. 9, 1680.
    v. Christian,[3] b. May 16, 1683; m. 1st, William Sampson, of Newbury; m. 2d, Feb. 24, 1712–3, James Smith, of Preston, Conn.
    vi. Penelope,[3] b. and d. Aug. 6, 1688.

4.   ISAAC[2] ELWELL (*Robert*[1]), bapt. at Salem, 27(12)1641-2, a sea-captain, married Mehitabel, daughter of Thomas and Mary (Greenaway) Millett, who was born at Dorchester 11(1)1641; she died in Gloucester, Sept. 28, 1699.   He married second, Dec. 16, 1702, Mrs. Mary (Prince) Rowe, daughter of Thomas Prince, and widow of Hugh Rowe; she died March 3, 1723, aged about 65 years.   He resided in Gloucester, on what is now known as High street.   He joined with the other sons-in-law and children of Thomas Millett in an agreement about the division of property, Sept. 27, 1682.   He sold to his son, Joshua Elwell, cordwainer, one acre of land at Gloucester, May 21, 1709, his wife Mary joining in the deed.   He died Oct. 14, 1715.

Administration on his estate was granted to his second son, Joshua Elwell (the eldest son having declined the trust), March 11, 1722-3.   Distribution was made to the children in due time; to Eleazer, the oldest son; to Joshua Elwell, Abigail Stover, Joanna Tucker, Bethia Urin, and Jemima Elwell.   Eleazer waived his claim to possession, and allowed Joshua to take the estate, and pay the other children their portions in money.

Children:

14.   i. ISAAC,[3] b. Jan. 15, 1666-7; drowned Jan. 5, 1690-1; admin. on his estate granted to Ezekiel Collins in favor of his brothers and sisters, Jan. 2, 1709-10.
ii. JANE,[3] b. Nov. 21, 1668.
15.   iii. JONATHAN,[3] b. Oct. 21, 1670.
16.   iv. ELEAZER,[3] b. July 16, 1673.
v. ABIGAIL,[3] b. April 13, 1676.
17.   vi. DAVID,[3] b. March 10, 1678-9.
vii. BETHIAH,[3] b. April 5, 1682; m. 1st, Jan. 17, 1705, Abraham Rowe; m. 2d, Jan. 26, 1720-1, Peter Uram.
viii. HANNAH[3] [Joanna] b. Feb. 4, 1687, twin; m. —— Tucker.
·18.   ix. JOSHUA,[3] b. Feb. 4, 1687, twin.
x. JEMIMA,[3] named in the administration papers; one Jemima Elwell m. Dec. 24, 1724, William Barnes; another m. Oct. 29, 1729, John Pool.

5.   JOSIAH[2] ELWELL (*Robert*[1]), born at Salem about 1644; married first, in Boston, June 15, 1666, Mary, daughter of John Collins; after his death she married second, 2(12)1679, John Cook, who was appointed joint administrator with her of Mr. Elwell's estate, 29(1)1681.   She survived him, and married third, Capt. James Davis.   She died March 9, 1725, aged 79.

The following interesting paper is on file at Salem:

"Settlement of the estate of —— Elwell late of Gloucester deceased. August 6th, 1717.

Cla[im] of the Estate of Widdow Elwell the Condition she was left in with 5 children; the Eldest abt 6 yeers old; & y[e] last one not borne:

Covenant and agreed Between Mary Elwell allias Davis on the one part Mother to Ellias Elwell both of Glocester on the other part, Witnesseth—that Mary Elwell now Davis Widdow; is to Injoy , the house that she now lives in, with one third of the Land Joyning to y House & one third of the Land below the Highway dureing her naturall life & returne what Puter platters that belonged to the father of the s[d] Ellias; & this is of all agreement between the mother & the Son as witness theire names. Moreover before signing it is agreed that y s[d] Ellias is to cleer his s[d] mother from his sister Dorcas from any demands in the s[d] Land & Household Stuff; the s[d] Whidow not to make strip & wast upon the s[d] Estate; agreed by both partyes that m[r] Ezekiel Collins; Samuell Stevens; & Phillemon Warner—shall be the partyes to lot out

the Land between the s⁴ Widdow & her son Ellias. and boath partyes
to Sett & rest contended what the above s⁴ Committee shall doe: as
Witness theire hand this Angst. 6th: 1717.

her
MARY   DAVIS
marke
ELIAS ELWELL."

Signed & Sealed & Deliver
in the prsence of Thomas Manning Thomas Choate

Children:

i. DORCAS,³ b. June 18, 1686; m. Nov. 8, 1686, John Babson. The cele-
brated historian of Gloucester, Mr. John J. Babson, is a descendant
of this couple.
19. ii. ELIAS.³ b. Oct. 16, 1668.
20. iii. NEHEMIAH,³ b. Dec. 21, 1671.
21. iv. WILLIAM.³ b. July 5, 1674.
v. JOSIAH.³ b. Dec. 21, 1676: d. Dec. 5, 1716.
Jane Elwell. widow, ae. about 45 years, d. April 5, 1723. Was she
the wife of this Josiah?

6. JOSEPH² ELWELL. (*Robert*¹). born in Salem or Gloucester. about 1619;
a fisherman; deposed in 1672, being about 23 years old; married,
June 22. 1669. Mary, daughter of Osman Dutch. a sister of the
wife of his brother Samuel. Perhaps she is the Mary Elwell who
died March 25. 1680.

Dec. 12, 1679. they sold a large tract of land at Cape Anne,
adjoining that of his father-in-law, to John Turner, of Salem, mer-
chant.

Children:

22. i. HEZEKIAH,³ b. June 2, 1670.
23. ii. JOSEPH,³ b. Aug. 19. 1672.
24. iii. SAMUEL,³ b. June 8, 1675.
25. iv. BENJAMIN,³ b. Sept. 13, 1678.

7. THOMAS² ELWELL (*Robert*¹). born in Gloucester. Nov. 21. 1651. married Nov. 23. 1675. Sarah, daughter of William Bassett, of Lynn;
she was remembered in her father's will, dated Feb. 10, 1701,
proved May 22, 1703.

No transfers of land or other traces of this couple are found in
the records of Essex County. Mass.. further than the register, at
Gloucester, of the births of the first five children, mentioned below;
it has therefore seemed probable that the family removed to some
distant section.

The people of Lynn had, some years before this time, sent many
pioneers to Long Island: Southampton, and other towns having
been largely made up of Lynn emigrants. It would not seem
strange, therefore, if we should find Thomas Elwell and his Lynn
wife joining in some such movement. West Jersey was then
developing: and not a few Massachusetts men entered into it, along
with the Quakers and other settlers.

The following documents on file at Trenton, N. J., confirm this
theory to a remarkable degree:

Salem County, New Jersey, Deeds, Liber No. 6. p. 243.

"Benjamin Acton to Thomas Elwell: 110 Acres of Land." * *

"For and in consideration of the sum of Eleven pounds currt. silver
money of y⁰ s⁴ prvince. in hand paid by Thomas Elwell. late of New
England & now of Salem Towne & County afores⁴ Weaver. at or before
the sealing & delivery hereof: the Receipt whereof is hereby Acknow-

ledged: As also for divers other good Causes & Considerations him
thereunto moveing. He the s⁴ Benjamin hath Granted. Bargained.
Sold. Aliened Enfeoffed & confirmed And by these prsents Doth Grant.
Bargain. Sell. Alien Enfeoffe & Confirme unto him the s⁴ Thomas
Elwell his heires & Agts. for ever, one hundred & Tenn Acres of Land.
Marsh & Swamps (be it more or less) being pte a peell of y⁰ s⁴ Tenn
Thousand Acres & is pte of y⁰ s⁴ 1500: acres before menconed & is butt-
ted & bounded follow⁽ᵗʰ⁾ vize⁴. Beginning at a White Oake Tree markt
T. E. standing on Nicomus Branch, at the uper end of branceses oald
ffeild. ffrom thence, 47. Rodd. North East. to a White Oake markt. T. E.
from thence: 44 Rodd. East to a Redd Oake markt T. E. from thence:
171. Rodd. Southwest to y⁰ line of Thomas Piles. 10000: Acres of Land.
From thence Southwest alonge y⁰ s⁴ line 112 Rodd. to the Corner Tree
of the s⁴ Tract of 10000 acres. from thence downe y⁰ sd. branch to y⁰
first menconed Tree * * * * y⁰ 6ᵗʰ day of 9 b⁰. A D. 1698 * * * *
Recorded y⁰ 8ᵗʰ of x b⁰ 1698."

In the name of God Amen. I Thomas Alewell Sen⁰ of Pilegrove
precinct in the county of Salem in the province of Nova Cesaria or West
Jersey carpenter being sick & weak of body but of sound and perfect
memory Praysed be given to the Almighty God for the same & caleing
to mind the unccartainty of this Life and the Ccartainty of Death Doe
Make and Ordaine this my Last will & Testamt. Revoking and Disan-
nulling all former will or Wills by me made Either by word of mouth or
in writing——

Imps: I give and bequeath my soul to Almighty God that gave it to
me and my body to the earth to be Deasently buryed at the Discretion
of my Execcutrx and execut⁰ hereafter named—

2ᵈˡʸ I desire that all my Just debts and Legacies be paid and
satisfied:

3⁴ˡʸ. I give and bequeath unto my Deare and Loving wife Sarah
Alewell all my Land and plantation where I now Live for and Dureing
her Naturall Life and after her Decease: I give The s⁴. Land and plantation unto my sonne Samuel Alewell his heirs & Assignes for ever. Alsoe
I give and bequeath unto my Dear & Loveing wife all my Movables both
within Doores and without for and Dureing her Naturall life and after
her Decease unto my three Daughters Sarah Walling, Mary Nickolds
and Elizabeth Alewell to be Equally Devided between them.

4ᵗʰˡʸ: I Give and bequeath unto son Thomas Alewell the sum of two
pounds Cur⁴ money of the s⁴ province.

5ᵗʰˡʸ. I give and bequeath to my son William Alewell the sum of two
pounds Cur⁴. money of the s⁴ province.

6ᵗʰˡʸ. I Give and bequeath unto my son John Elwell the sum of one
pound Cur⁴ money of y⁰ s⁴ province to be paid them when my son Samuell
shall Attaine to the Age of twenty one yeares——

7ᵗʰˡʸ. I ordaine and appoynt my Dear and Loveing wife Sarah Alewell
and my Son Samuel Alewell to be my Execcutrix and Execut⁰ of this my
Last will and Testamt to see it pformed alsoe I doe Authorise and Impower my s⁴ Execcutrix and Execut⁰ to make over and convey unto my
son-in-law Thomas Walling unto his heires and Assignes forever sixteen
Acres of land where he now Liveth on which was pchased of me. In
Witness whereof I have hereunto sett my hand and Seale this 25: day
of Aprill Anno Dom 1706—

his
THOMAS | ꞏ | ALEWELL
mark

Signed: Sealed: Published
and Declared this to be his
Last Will and Testament
in the prsence of uss—
    Joseph White
    Edward Hoard   her
                 Mary X Hoard
                     mark
                 Samⁱⁱ Hodges

Proved April 20, 1707.

With this is filed

An Inventory of the Goods and Catcles of Tho. Elweall Deceased Apraised by Josep Whitte and William Hall this 27 d. of yᵉ 3 ᵐᵒ 1706.

To his wearing Aperall	£2-10-0
" fether bed and furnetor: old at	5-0-0
" a peareceall of Nailes	1-10-0
" 2 gunnes att	2-10-0
" 11 pound wole att	0-17-0
" a perceal of Toyarne	0-12-0
" sum old Puter	1-0-0
" a perceall of old milk vesseles old Tubes and botcles	0-15-0
" 3 old Iron pottes	
" frienpann	3-10-0
" 2 peare Raikes 1 spitt 2 pear pott hocks	
" 1 beane Skellett 1 peare fler shovel and Tongues all att	
" aperceall Carpenters toles Iron wedges and mall Ring	2-10-0
" aperceall of clothin yᵉ lome with the lome and geeres att	3-0-0
" 1 old Grind Stone att	0-5-0
" 5 bagges att	1-5-0
" 1 plane and joiner att	0-18-0
" 13 yong swine at 5s ppeas	3-05-0
" 2 chests bocks at	0-10-0
" 1 old tabeall att	0-2-6
" 2 yoes and lambes at	1-1-0
" 1 maire att	1-0-0
" 1 corne one the ground and flacks:	5-0-0
" 2 hides att	0-10-0
" 14 Neate Cattcle att	31-0-0
	£70-13-6

Children :

i. SARAH.³ b. Aug. 24, 1676.
26. ii. THOMAS.³ b. April 26, 1678.
iii. MARY,³ b. March 13, 1679-80.
27. iv. WILLIAM.³ b. April 8, 1682.
v. ELISHAH³ [ELIZABETH³], b. May 30, 1684.
28. vi. JOHN,³ named in his father's will.
29. vii. SAMUEL,³ named in his father's will; under age in 1706.

[NOTE.—While there is no absolute evidence to prove that the Thomas Elwell, born at Gloucester Nov. 21, 1654, is the identical person who removed from some place in "New England" to Salem county, New Jersey, and who there bought land as here specified, in the year 1698—no positive, documentary record having been found to show this: who can question the probable evidence here presented? In no other region in New England do we find an Elwell family at that period, save at Gloucester, Mass. The age of the Gloucester Thomas Elwell corresponds with the movements of the New Jersey settler: the names of the wife and five of the seven children are identical; the names of succeeding generations are largely those commonly used in the Gloucester families; and the movement of people from Lynn (where Thomas, of Gloucester, had married), to Long Island, is a pointer in the direction of the Fenwick Colony, which attracted quite a number of settlers from Eastern plantations. Altogether, the theory adopted by the compiler seems so very probable that no one need hesitate to adopt it as substantially proven.—EDITOR.]

Thomas Shourds, in his History of Fenwick's Colony, says: "The Elwell Family of this county, particularly those who have resided in the township of Pittsgrove, have had a large influence, both in religious and civil society." He gives a confused tradition as to the origin of the family, stating that Jacob, of whom he speaks highly, was the immigrant ancestor; this is altogether dissipated by the will of Jacob's father, Samuel, No. 29.

R. G. Johnson, in his History of Salem, N. J., says: "The Baptist Church in Pitts Grove was founded about the year 1743 by several families who emigrated from New England; such were the Reeds, Elwells, Cheesmans, Paullins and Wallaces."

8. SAMUEL[3] ELWELL (*Samuel*,[2] *Robert*[1]), born at Gloucester, March 14, 1659. He sold to Samuel Bishop of Ipswich, July 25, 1684, his house and land willed to him by his grandfather, Robert Elwell, Sr., and may be believed to have been living in 1695, when his father is called senior in a deed. No further note of him has come to hand.

9. JACOB[3] ELWELL (*Samuel*,[2] *Robert*[1]), born at Gloucester, Aug. 10, 1662; married July 5, 1686, Abigail, daughter of William Vincent (or Vinson, as it was commonly pronounced and written). She was born May 8, 1668. They sold, Sept. 1, 1695, to John Emerson, Jr., clerk, a tract of land at Sandy Bar, Gloucester, which fell to William Vinson, deceased.

He was killed in the French and Indian war, at Cape Sable, May 2, 1710. [Gloucester Records.] The widow sold lands in 1714 and 1728.

Children:

    i. BENJAMIN,[4] b. July 6, 1686; d. Sept. 11, 1694.
    ii. RACHEL,[4] b. Feb. 21, 1688; m. Peter Lurvey.
    iii. ABIGAIL,[4] b. Jan. 30, 1690.
    iv. SARAH,[4] b. Feb. 8, 1692.
    v. JACOB, b. March 26, 1695; d. Sept. 29, 1713.
    vi. HANNAH,[4] b. May 6, 1697; m. John Brown, of Falmouth, Me. William Elwell of Gloucester, yeoman: John Brown of Falmouth, yeoman, and Hannah Brown, alias Elwell, his wife; the said William Elwell and Hannah Elwell being heirs of Abigail Elwell, alias Vinson and of William Vinson, their grandfather; and Mary Elwell, widow, relict of Vinson Elwell, deceased, and guardian to his children; made an agreement concerning the division of the Vinson and Elwell property to which they were heirs, Jan. 23, 1745.
30. vii. VINSON,[4] b. July 15, 1700.
    viii. LYDIA,[4] b. Dec. 10, 1702.
31. ix. WILLIAM,[4] b. April 6, 1705.
    x. MARY,[4] b. Jan. 29, 1708.

10. ROBERT[3] ELWELL (*Samuel*,[2] *Robert*[1]), born at Gloucester, Dec. 13, 1664; fisherman and sea captain; married Oct. 12, 1687, Sarah, daughter of James Gardner. He sold to William Stevens of Gloucester, ship carpenter, Dec. 16, 1700, a parcel of land at Eastern Point, given him by his grandfather, Robert Elwell. Other portions of that legacy he sold in 1702 and 1712. He sold certain lands and privileges in Gloucester to his son Robert, in 1712–13. He removed to Kittery, Me., and there sold all his property and rights in Gloucester to his children, as follows: to Samuel Elwell of Gloucester, fisherman: to Joseph and John Elwell of Biddeford, husbandmen: to Hannah, the wife of Nathaniel Duriel, and Sarah, the wife of Robert Edgecomb of Biddeford: dated Sept. 24, 1730.

Children:

32. i. ROBERT,[4] b. Sept. 18, 1688.
    ii. SARAH,[4] b. and d. in 1692.
    iii. HANNAH,[4] b. Jan. 25, 1694; m. Nathaniel Durriel of Biddeford, Me.
33. iv. SAMUEL,[4] b. May 25, 1697.

34.   v. BENJAMIN,[4] b. March 17, 1790.
    vi. SARAH,[4] b. Jan. 28, 1793; m. Robert Edgecombe of Biddeford, Me.
35.   vii. JOSEPH,[4] b. Aug. 11, 1795.
36.   viii. JOHN,[4] b. Dec. 28, 1708.
    ix. JEMIMAH,[4] b. May 11, 1712; d. Dec. 26, 1714.

11. EBENEZER[3] ELWELL (*Samuel*,[2] *Robert*[1]), born at Gloucester, Feb. 29, 1670–1; married Jan. 2, 1695, Jean ———.
    He had a grant of land to set his house upon, between his brother Thomas Elwell and Abraham Robinson.
    Children:
      i. CHARLES,[4] b. and d. in 1695.
      ii. JEAN,[4] b. May 31, 1696.
      iii. PENELOPE,[4] b. Jan. 24, 1697–98.
      iv. JOSEPH,[4] b. July 22, 1699; d. May 9, 1721.
      v. EBENEZER,[4] b. March 1, 1702; d. at sea in June, 1720.
      vi. SUSANNA,[4] b. July 5, 1709.
      vii. ANNA,[4] b. April 15, 1711.

13. JOHN[3] ELWELL (*John*,[2] *Robert*[1]), born at Gloucester, Oct. 14, 1668; a sea captain; married Mary, daughter of Abraham Robinson, born Aug. 20, 1669. He married second, Jan. 7, 1709, Mary Joslyn.
    He resided in Gloucester; was living there in 1729, as we learn from a deed of land that year.
    Children:
37.   i. JOHN,[4] b. March 16, 1690.
    ii. MARY,[4] b. Oct. 8, 1695.
    iii. ABIGAIL,[4] b. Aug. 6, 1697.
    iv. RACHEL,[4] b. June 14, 1699.
    v. DEBORAH,[4] b. Aug. 7, 1702.
38.   vi. ANDREW,[4] b. April 22, 1704.
    vii. DORCAS,[4] b. June 24, 1706.
39.   viii. ABRAHAM,[4] b. Dec. 16, 1710.
    ix. LUCY,[4] b. July 3, 1714.

15. JONATHAN[3] ELWELL (*Isaac*,[2] *Robert*[1]), born at Gloucester, Oct. 21, 1670; married first, Abigail ———; second, Lydia, daughter of Thomas Sallows, of Beverly.
    He was a sailor and fisherman. He bought a tract of land on the road from Gloucester to Beverly of John Hill or Hull of Manchester, weaver, and Miriam his wife, June 20, 1723; and, in partnership with William Barnes, he bought of William and Ruth Elwell, Feb. 6, 1733, four acres in Gloucester. He and his wife Abigail sold the first named premises Nov. 27, 1727, to John Sallis (Sallows). His first wife appears to have died in 1729; for we have the record of the birth of her son Nathaniel in that year, and the birth of another son Nathaniel of the wife Lydia in 1730. Benjamin Ryland and Lydia Ober testified Aug. 31, 1747, that they saw Thomas Sallows, late of Beverly, execute a deed of sale of his house and lands to his daughter, Lydia Elwell, in January, February or March last, and that the deed was antedated at the request of said Sallows.
    Administration on the estate of Jonathan and Lydia Elwell was granted March 6, 1748, to their son-in-law Thomas Cary. He is called "late of Gloucester"; she, "late of Beverly." In June, 1752, the estate was divided to the son Nathaniel, the heirs of the daughter Lydia Cary, and the daughters Anna and Lucy.

Children :

　i. ABIGAIL,[4] b. July 16, 1727.
　ii. NATHANIEL,[4] b. June 15, 1729.
40.　iii. NATHANIEL,[4] b. in June. 1730.
　iv. ANNA,[4] b. in December, 1732; m. John Sallows. "John Sallows, mariner, and Anna Swallows, seamster, of Beverly, sold to Zebedee Day of Gloucester, mason, all their interest in the estate of their father, Jonathan Elwell. Dec. 19, 1755.
　v. LUCY,[4] named in probate papers.

16.　ELEAZER[3] ELWELL (*Isaac,*[2] *Robert*[1]), born at Gloucester, July 16, 1675 ; a cordwainer ; married Jan. 21, 1697. Eme, daughter of Nicholas Denning. May 21, 1729, a deposition was made by Richard and John Pearce, to the effect that " Agnes Doliber, Eme Elwell, Eliza Paine, Nicholas Denning and George Denning were all the reputed children of Eme Browne, daughter of John Browne and wife of Nicholas Denning who formerly lived at New Harbour at the Eastward, near Pemaquid." In a deed of the Pearces, made about that date, New Harbour is said to be in Nova Scotia ; so unsettled were the bounds of the Eastern colonies at that period.
　　Children :

41.　i. JONATHAN,[4] b. Feb. 10, 1698.
　ii. MEHETABEL,[4] b. Oct. 11, 1700.
42.　iii. DAVID,[4] b. May 2, 1703.
43.　iv. PAINE,[4] b. Aug. 15, 1707.
　v. ABIGAIL,[4] b. Aug. 13, 1714.

17.　DAVID[3] ELWELL (*Isaac,*[2] *Robert*[1]), born at Gloucester, March 10, 1678–9 ; a fisherman ; married October 26, 1727. Sarah Mariner. He bought a tract of land in Gloucester of John Elwell, Feb. 20, 1728–29, and sold two tracts Oct. 18, 1732.
　　Children :

44.　i. DAVID,[4] b. Dec. 17. 1728.
　ii. SARAH,[4] b. July. 1730.
　iii. RACHEL,[4] b. in March. 1732.

18.　JOSHUA[3] ELWELL (*Isaac,*[2] *Robert*[1]), born at Gloucester ; fisherman ; married Dec. 24. 1709. Alice Low. She died Jan. 8, 1717. He married second, Nov. 28, 1717. Abigail, daughter of Thomas Riggs, Jr., and Ann Wheeler of Salisbury, his wife. He sold lands in 1719 and 1724.
　　Children :

　i. BETHIAH,[4] b. Dec. 10. 1710.
　ii. ALICE,[4] b. April 21, 1712.
45.　iii. ISAAC,[4] b. Oct. 31. 1714.
46.　iv. JOSHUA,[4] b. Dec. 16, 1716.
·47.　v. THOMAS,[4] b. Aug. 18, 1718.
　vi. MOSES,[4] b. Sept. 1, 1720 ; d. March 19, 1721.
　vii. ANN,[4] b. June 23, 1722.
　viii. SARAH,[4] b. Aug. 11, 1725.
48.　ix. MARK,[4] b. Sept. 17. 1730.
49.　x. AARON,[4] b. Oct. 16. 1732.
　xi. MEHETABLE,[4] b. Dec. 16, 1735.

19.　ELIAS[3] ELWELL (*Josiah,*[2] *Robert*[1]), born at Gloucester. Oct. 16, 1668 ; sea captain ; married Nov. 12. 1690. Dorcas, daughter of Deacon Thomas Lowe of Ipswich. He sold land at the Cape to John Smith, Nov. 30, 1710 ; bought a tract at Little Good Harbour marsh, Jan. 12, 1718–19. He and his brother Josiah bought the rights of John Babson and Dorcas his wife to the estate of their father, Josiah Elwell, deceased, April 20, 1710. May 25, 1734, he conveyed land to his son Elias.

He bought a house and land in Gloucester of Ezekiel Collins, Sept. 30, 1691; a piece of marsh land of widow Hadley, Jan. 12, 1718–19.

His will was proved Aug. 1, 1737; names all the children except the first Nehemiah and the daughter Hannah. His inventory mentions among other items "One small island in the harbour, called five pound island," which was appraised at twenty pounds. To his two young children, Daniel and Nehemiah, he bequeathed house lots of equivalent value to those he had previously given the older children; to his sons William, Josiah and Joseph, and to his daughter Experience he gave portions; and equal amounts to the children of his daughter Dorcas Ellery; all the rest of his estate he gave to his wife, "at her dispose in life and at her Death," and appointed her his executrix. The property was quite large.

Children:

i. EXPERIENCE,[4] b. June 16, 1691.
ii. DORCAS,[4] b. Sept. 16, 1695.
50. iii. WILLIAM,[4] b. May 8, 1698.
iv. NEHEMIAH,[4] b. April. 1701; d. July 31, 1716, at Prospect Harbour, beyond Cape Sable.
51. v. JOSIAH,[4] b. July 25, 1703.
52. vi. ELIAS,[4] b. July 30, 1709.
53. vii. DANIEL,[4] b. Feb. 27, 1712.
viii. HANNAH,[4] bapt. June 16, 1723.
54. ix. NEHEMIAH,[4] named in his father's will.

22. HEZEKIAH[3] ELWELL (*Joseph*,[2] *Robert*[1]), born at Gloucester, June 2, 1670; married Elizabeth, daughter of John and Deborah Fennicke (Fenwick). Resided at Kittery, Me. He died, and his widow conveyed the homestead to her son-in-law, Richard Clembole, June 26, 1749.

Children:

i. ANNE,[4] b. Aug. 12, 1693; m. (intention recorded March 13, 1735) Richard Clambole.
ii. MARY,[4] b. Feb. 17, 1696; m. Jan. 18, 1718, William [More].
iii. DEBORAH,[4] b. Jan. 6, 1702; m. Dec. 24, 1723, Daniel Williams.
iv. ELIZABETH,[4] b. July 10, 1705; m. (intention) May 28, 1726, Robert Elwell, of Biddeford; m. Dec. 6, 1728, Joseph Elwell of Biddeford. Eight children.

Perhaps Sarah Elwell, who intended marriage with Abraham Weeks at Kittery, Feb. 13, 1730–31, was another child.

25. BENJAMIN[3] ELWELL of Kittery, and Mary Grover of York, intentions Oct. 2, 1731, married Dec. 21, 1731, at York [believed to be Benjamin[2] (*Joseph*,[2] *Robert*[1])].

26. THOMAS[3] ELWELL (*Thomas*,[2] *Robert*[1]), born at Gloucester, April 26, 1678; married Susanna ———.

He went to New Jersey with his father and settled.

Thomas Elwell, Jr., husbandman, bought land in Salem County, N. J., Jan. 19, 1699.

Thomas Ellewell June[r] of Pilegrove, county of Salem, province of West Jersey, carpenter, bought of George Gerrett of the same, for five pounds and ten shillings, twenty five acres of land, Beginning at an ash Tree standinge by Chestnut Run mark[it] with y[e] Letters S. B. G. G. from Thence north and By West Twenty five Rod and a halfe to a Red oke mark[it] T E From Thence north East a little notherly two hundred Rod To a W[t] oke mark[it] T E From Thence South East Twenty Rod to a W[t] oke mark[it] T E From Thence South West to y[e] first menc'oned Tree * * * twenty forth day of august anno: Dom[i] 1701."

Thomas Elwell of Piles Grove Precincts in the county of Salem, made will Aug. 14, 1722. Bequeathed the plantation where he dwelt to his two sons, Thomas and Josiah Elwell, his wife Susannah to have life use of the premises; five pounds to each of the residue of his children; his twenty-five acres of cedar swamp lying near the branches of the Morr River to his son Thomas. Prob. Dec. 17, 1724.—(Salem Co., N. J., Wills, Lib. 2, p. 282.)

Certificate of the survey of a tract of land by order of Thomas and Josiah Elwell, May 6, 1731, which Thomas Elwell, deceased, purchased Jan. 19, 1699.—(From MS book of Rev. Thomas Killingsworth, pastor Cohansey Baptist Church, and judge of Salem County, N. J., court.)

Children :

55. i. THOMAS.[4]
56. ii. JOSIAH.[4]

[Other children, not recorded, referred to in the will as "*the residue of my children*."]

[Mary Elwell, of Salem, was licensed to marry John Crane, of Burlington, Feb. 19, 1727.

Sarah Elwell and Henry Vanmeter, of Salem, were licensed to marry Sept. 4, 1727.]

27. WILLIAM[3] ELWELL (*Thomas,[2] Robert[1]*), born at Gloucester, April 8, 1682 ; married in New Jersey a wife whose name has not yet been ascertained by the writer, and died in the year 1728, leaving a family of four children. He made his will 21 (11) 1728-9, which was admitted to probate Feb. 17 following, bequeathing his estate to his wife, and to his children John, William, Sarah and Hannah. He appointed his brother, Samuel Elwell, executor.

Children :

57. i. JOHN.[4]
58. ii. WILLIAM.[4]
iii. SARAH.[4]
iv. HANNAH.[4]

28. JOHN[3] ELWELL (*Thomas,[2] Robert[1]*), place and date of birth unknown to the writer, was licensed to marry, March 24, 1727, Rachel Garrison. Both were residents of Salem, Salem County, New Jersey. Probably his second marriage. The following abstract of his will is all we find concerning this family. No actual evidence makes it certain that the John referred to in the will of Thomas, Sr., is the husband of Rachel ; but probability leads us to place the two records in line.

John Elwell, of Pilesgrove, county of Salem, in the Western Division in the province of West Jersey, carpenter, made will April 15, 1758, probated May 2, 1758. He bequeathed his estate to his wife Rachel, son John Elwell, daughters Elizabeth Holton, Rachel Newman and Esther Elwell, and grandson Andrew Lock.

Children :

59. i. John.[4]
     ii. Elizabeth,[4] licensed to marry John Holton of Salem, Jan. 25, 1745.
     iii. Rachel,[4] m. —— Newman.
     iv. Esther,[4] licensed to marry Adam Ruderford of Pilesgrove, Aug. 21, 1761.

29. Samuel[3] Elwell (*Thomas,*[2] *Robert*[1]), born probably in New Jersey about 1688, is known to the writer only through the Probate Records at Trenton, N. J. Samuel Elwell, of the township of Pilesgrove, in the county of Salem and Western Division of the Province of New Jersey, yeoman, made will Jan. 5, 1739–40. Wife Tamzon to have use of his plantation for life, or as long as she would remain his widow ; to his son Jacob Elwell he gave his grist-mill and the land whereon he now liveth, which is sixty acres of land ; to son Samuel Elwell one hundred acres of land in the best end of his plantation, upon the death of his widow ; to his son Abraham the remainder of the plantation ; to daughter Rachel Brick, wife of William Brick, a portion ; to daughter Susanna Ray, wife unto John Ray ; to daughters Elizabeth and Tamzon Elwell ; another child expected. Proved Feb. 16, 1739–40.
     Children :

60. i. Jacob,[4] one of the constituent members of the Baptist Church of Pittsgrove in 1743.
61. ii. Samuel.[4]
62. iii. Abraham.[4]
     iv. Rachel,[4] licensed to marry William Brick, June 1, 1731.
     v. Susanna,[4] m. John Ray.
     vi. Elizabeth.[4]
     vii. Tamzon.[4]
     viii. ?

30. Vinson[4] Elwell (*Jacob,*[3] *Samuel,*[2] *Robert*[1]), born at Gloucester, July 15, 1700 ; married Dec. 21, 1732, Mary Lurvey. He died before 1745, when his widow, as guardian of his children, conveyed their rights in lands inherited from the Vinson (Vincent) and Elwell families. (See under No. 9.)
     Children :

     i. Vinson,[5] b. July 14, 1733.
     ii. Rachel,[5] b. Oct. 25, 1735 ; m. May 8, 1757, William Hutchings.
     iii. Mary,[5] b. Feb. 28, 1738.
     iv. Lydia,[5] b. Feb. 6, 1739 ; d. in 1742.
     v. Lydia,[5] b. June 26, 1743.

31. William[4] Elwell (*Jacob,*[3] *Samuel,*[2] *Robert*[1]), yeoman, born at Gloucester, April 6, 1705 ; married Elizabeth ——.
     See agreement for division of property made with his sisters, under 9, vi., *ante.*
          It has been inferred from a number of facts that this is the William Elwell who was an early settler of Meduncook (Friendship), Me.
     Children :

     i. Jacob,[5] b. Nov. 15, 1729.
     ii. Elizabeth,[5] b. Jan. 10, 1739.
     iii. William,[5] b. June 21, 1742.

32. ROBERT⁴ ELWELL (*Robert,*³ *Samuel,*² *Robert*¹). born at Gloucester,
Sept. 18. 1688; married Nov. 1, 1713. Jemima, daughter of John
Smith. "He died at Ipswich under the doctor's hands. Mr. Wallis,"
June 2, 1715.

John Smith of Gloucester. yeoman, conveyed his property to his
sons Daniel and Jonathan Smith. May 12. 1719. they to pay certain amounts to his daughters. Rebecca. wife of Elisha Corney,
Elizabeth Smith and Jemima Elwell; to his daughter-in-law,
Susanna Smith, and her son John Smith. his grandson; and to his
grandson John Corney.

Child:

    i. JONATHAN,⁵ b. April 14. 1714; bapt. Oct. 31. 1725; seems to be the
      man who married. March 28, 1737. Abigail. dau. of Samuel Stevens,
      and had sons Jonathan, Robert, Samuel and William. and several
      daughters. He d. March 10. æ. 94.

33. SAMUEL⁴ ELWELL (*Robert,*³ *Samuel,*² *Robert*¹). born at Gloucester,
May 25. 1697; married April 27. 1718. Rebecca Brown. Administration on his estate was granted to his son Samuel. May 11. 1712.
Administration on the estate of Samuel Elwell was granted May
25, 1747, to his widow Abigail; whether the same estate or
another. deponent saith not.

Children:

    i. SAMUEL,⁵ b. Oct. 5, 1718.
    ii. ROBERT,⁵ b. Nov. 11, 1720.
    iii. DAVID,⁵ b. Sept. 29, 1723.
    iv. REBECCA,⁶ b. Dec. 12. 1725.
    v. SARAH,⁵ b. Feb. 6, 1727.
    vi. LOWIS⁵ (Louisa?). b. March 9, 1731.
    vii. DAVID,⁵ b. Aug. 4. 1733.
    viii. DORCAS,⁵ b. July 20, 1735.
    ix. BENJAMIN,⁵ b. April 15, 1737.

37. JOHN⁴ ELWELL (*John,*³ *John,*² *Robert*¹). born at Gloucester. March
16. 1690; married December 15, 1712, Lydia, daughter of ———
Giddings.

Capt. John Elwell's estate was probated June 21, 1766, amount-
ing to £186:3:6, naming wife Ruth.

Children:

    i. An Infant, b. and d. in 1714.
    ii. LYDIA,⁵ b. Oct. 25, 1715.
    iii. JOHN,⁵ b. July 3, 1718.
    iv. ZEBULON,⁵ b. May 8, 1721.
    v. MARY,⁵ b. Dec. 23, 1723.

38. ANDREW⁴ ELWELL (*John,*³ *John,*² *Robert*¹). born at Gloucester. April
22, 1704; a fisherman; married Dec. 12, 1723, Lydia Gearing.
He bought a dwelling house and lane of Andrew Robinson, Jan. 6,
1726–7.

Children:

    i. RACHEL,⁵ b. July 23, 1724.
    ii. LYDIA,⁵ b. July 17. 1726.
    iii. ANDREW,⁵ b. April 1, 1730.
    iv. ABRAHAM,⁵ b. Nov. 4, 1733.
    v. ISAAC,⁵ b. July 13, 1735.
    vi. ABIGAIL,⁵ b. July 4, 1737.

43. PAINE[4] ELWELL (*Eleazer,[3] Isaac,[2] Robert[1]*), born at Gloucester, Aug. 15, 1707.

Children :

  i. SARAH.[5]
  ii. PAINE.[5] b. Jan. 27, 1735.
  iii. SARAH,[5] b. May 22, 1739.
  iv. MARY,[5] b. Aug. 13, 1741.

45. ISAAC[4] ELWELL (*Joshua,[3] Isaac,[2] Robert[1]*), born at Gloucester, Oct. 31, 1714; married Nov. 15, 1738, Susanna Stanwood.

Children :

  i. ISAAC,[5] b. and d. in 1740.
  ii. SUSANNAH,[5] b. Aug. 13, 1741.
  iii. ISAAC,[5] b. July 2, 1743.
  iv. LUCY,[5] b. May 6, 1745.
  v. JOSHUA,[5] b. Sept. 15, 1748.
  vi. DAVID,[5] b. July 25, 1751.
  vii. SOLOMON,[5] b. June 1, 1753.
  viii. ELIAS,[5] b. Oct. 6, 1755.
  ix. ANNA,[5] b. Aug. 5, 1758.
  x. ALICE LOW,[5] b. Aug. 27, 1760.
  xi. BETTY,[5] b. Nov. 5, 1762.

·47. THOMAS[4] ELWELL (*Joshua,[3] Isaac,[2] Robert[1]*), born at Gloucester, Aug. 18, 1718; married first, October 22, 1740, Lucy Pierce; married second, in May, 1762, Elizabeth Stratton.

He is believed to be the man who bought land in Kingfield, Dec. 21, 1750; in Palmer, Sept. 7, 1753; and in Hardwick, where he continued to reside, May 2, 1758. He died Jan. 27, 1798. In his will, dated Dec. 30, 1784, proved Feb. 6, 1798, he mentions children of his first wife, Joshua, Thomas, John, Jonas, Jabez and Moses.

Children :

  i. THOMAS PIERCE,[5] b. Feb. 22, 1741.
  ii. JOSHUA.[5]
  iii. JOHN,[5] bapt. Oct. 8, 1758, at Hardwick.
  iv. JONAS,[5] b. July 16, 1759.
  — v. JABEZ.[5]
  vi. MOSES.[5]
  vii. MARK,[5] b. Feb. 2, 1763.
  viii. ANNA,[5] b. Aug. 14, 1764; m. June 20, 1787, Noah Moody of South Hadley.
  ix. DAVID,[5] b. June 1, 1766.
  x. [LUCIA RICE[5]].

48. MARK[4] ELWELL (*Joshua,[3] Isaac,[2] Robert[1]*), born at Gloucester, Sept. 17, 1730; became a farmer, at Dudley; married first, Mary Hibbard; married second, Aug. 29, 1774, Mrs. Dorothy (Lamb) White. He was called Lieutenant on Dudley Records at the time of his second marriage; residence, Killingly, Conn.

Children :

  i. MARK,[5] b. Feb. 25, 1777.
  ii. ABIEL,[5] b. May 16, 1781.
  iii. BENJAMIN,[5] b. Nov. 25, 1785. His son, William S. Elwell of Springfield, was an artist of repute.

50. WILLIAM[4] ELWELL (*Elias,[3] Josiah,[2] Robert[1]*), born at Gloucester, May 8, 1698; married at Gloucester, Oct. 27, 1720, Elizabeth, daughter of Joseph and Deborah York. William Elwell, of Gloucester, mariner,

and Ruth, his wife, sold Aug. 1, 1726, to John Millett of the same, yeoman, a tract of land in Gloucester: they sold another tract to Edmund Grover, Jr., Oct. 9, 1736. They receipted, Dec. 6, 1732, for the portion of the estate of the late Joseph York, which fell to Ruth as one of his daughters.

51. JOSIAH[4] ELWELL (*Elias,[3] Josiah,[2] Robert[1]*), born at Gloucester, July 25, 1703; married ——— Lamer.
He made his will April 20, 1739, when bound to sea, giving one half his estate to his wife and the other half to his brother Elias.

52. ELIAS[4] ELWELL (*Elias,[3] Josiah,[2] Robert[1]*), b. at Gloucester, July 30, 1709; sea captain: married Abigail ———: to her he bequeathed his property by his will made in 1740, and proved in 1752. Resided at Gloucester.

53. DANIEL[4] ELWELL (*Elias,[3] Josiah,[2] Robert[1]*), born at Gloucester, Feb. 27, 1712; married Jan. 23, 1740, Mary Stanwood.
Child:
    i. DANIEL,[5] b. June 30, d. Nov. 4, 1741.

54. NEHEMIAH[4] ELWELL (*Elias,[3] Josiah,[2] Robert[1]*), born at Gloucester, Sept. 4, 1718; married Mary ———. He resided in Gosport, Eng., a few years, but returned to Gloucester, where he died; at least, his estate was administered upon by his wife in 1762.
Children:
    i. WILLIAM,[5] b. at Gosport, Eng., Jan. 31, 1747.
    ii. MARY,[5] b. Nov. 30, 1752.
    iii. ELIAS,[5] b. Oct. 31, 1755.
    iv. DORCAS,[5] b. Oct. 8, 1758.

55. THOMAS[4] ELWELL (*Thomas,[3] Thomas,[2] Robert[1]*). Administration on the estate of Thomas Elwell, late of Salem County, New Jersey, was granted to (his widow) Mary Elwell, Jan. 19, 1754.

57. JOHN[4] ELWELL (*William,[3] Thomas,[2] Robert[1]*),* born in Salem County, New Jersey, about 1717; married first, Abigail Sawtelle, who was born Feb. 13, 1722, and died July 31, 1765. He married a second and a third wife, whose names the writer has not been able to learn. He resided at Pittsgrove, N. J. He died about 1787. The following notes of his will have been made:

Notes of the Last Will and Testament of John Elwell, taken the 6th day of July, 1787.
Item: I give to my son Alexander Elwell 80 acres of land where he now lives, joining land of Samuel Elwell, Paullin, and the other part of my Plantation.
I give all the remaining of my Plantation to my sons Sawtel, Amariah, Even & Ephraim, to be equally Divided between them and if my son Ephraim should die before he comes to the age of twenty one years his part to be divided between his 3 brothers last mentioned.
I give to my daughter Luraniah a feather bed and bedding, a case of drawers and a small desk. And all the rest of my personal estate after my debts are paid I do order to be equally divided between my 3 sons and 2 daughters. And I do order the executors of this my last will and testament to put the part which will be coming to my son Ephraim to interest, and the interest to the use of

* The parentage of this man is not proved by complete documentary evidence; but many circumstances point to William as his father, and seem to warrant this arrangement of the line.—EDITOR.

bringing him up and his schooling. And I appoint my sons Sawtel, Amariah and Alexander Elwell Executors of this my last Will and Testament.

In Sept., 1795, a commission was appointed to divide the property according to the terms of the will.

Children :

i. Zachariah,[5] b. Feb. 27, 1739; d. young.
ii. Rebecca,[5] b. Feb. 7, 1741.
iii. Sawtelle,[5] b. Oct. 17, 1742.
iv. Rachel,[5] b. Sept. 8, 1744.
v. Henry,[5] b. April 21, 1746.
vi. Sarah,[5] b. March 13, 1750.
vii. Amariah,[5] b. June 6, 1753. He was a soldier in Anderson's company of the 3d Battalion, 2d Establishment of Continental troops, and also in the 1st Battalion of Salem militia.
viii. Elizabeth,[5] b. Nov. 23, 1754.
63. ix. Alexander,[5] b. July 22, 1756.
x. Evan,[5] b. April 6, 1758.
xi. Leubaney,[5] b. May 29, 1760.
xii. Ellis,[5] b. Feb. 20, 1763.
xiii. Ephraim,[5] b. April 21, 1785.

59. John[4] Elwell (John,[3] Thomas,[2] Robert[1]). [Probable pedigree.]
John Elwell, of Pittsgrove, county of Salem, New Jersey, made will Feb. 14, 1803, proved April 4, 1804; wife Elizabeth, son John Elwell, daughters Rebecca and Elizabeth Elwell.

John Elwell was a private in New York's company of the second battalion of militia from the town of Salem.

63. Alexander[5] Elwell (John,[4] William,[3] Thomas,[2] Robert[1]), born at Pittsgrove, N. J., July 22, 1756; married Sept. 26, 1782, Elizabeth Howes, born June 26, 1759, d. Aug. [2], 1822.

The inventory of the estate of Alexander Elwell, late of Pitts Grove in the county of Salem, taken Aug. 22, 1808, by Samuel Elwell, Senior, and Samuel Nelson, was presented Sept. 4, 1809, by Henry and Samuel Elwell, administrators.

Horses, Cattle, Sheep and Swine	\$172.25
Grain in the Ground and stack and hay in stack	63.00
Household Goods, kitchen furniture & farming utensils	228.00
Book Accounts	3.37
	\$466.66

Children :

i. Henry,[6] b. Oct. 16, 1783.
64. ii. Samuel S.,[6] b. Dec. 18, 1785.
iii. Charles,[6] b. March 31, 1788.
iv. John Howes,[6] b. March 26, 1790.
v. Joseph More,[6] b. Feb. 26, 1792.
vi. Mary,[6] } b. March 26, 1794.
vii. Robert,[6] {
viii. Jeremiah,[6] b. Sept. 21, 1797.

64. Samuel S.[6] Elwell (Alexander,[5] John,[4] William,[3] Thomas,[2] Robert[1]), born at Pittsgrove, N. J., Dec. 18, 1785; married Sept. 8, 1812, Anna Berryman, born Aug. 20, 1787, died Dec. 8, 1827. He resided at Philadelphia.

Children :

i. Elizabeth,[7] b. Aug. 1, 1813; d. Aug. 12, 1814.
ii. Sarah Ann,[7] b. Jan. 13, 1815; d. Aug. 23, 1820.
65. iii. Samuel Berryman,[7] b. Aug. 21, 1816.

iv. ALEXANDER D.,[8] b. and d. in 1818.
v. MARY ELLEN,[7] b. May 18, 1819; d. Nov. 12, 1851.
vi. REBECCA,[7] b. Feb. 8, 1821; d. Jan. 10, 1853.
vii. SARAH ANN,[7] b. Aug. 20, 1823; d. Dec. 26, 1824.
viii. HENRY COLEMAN,[7] b. March 21, 1825.
ix. ANN JEMIMA,[7] b. May 1, 1827; d. June 28, 1875.

65. SAMUEL[7] BERRYMAN ELWELL (*Samuel S.,[6] Alexander,[6] John,[4] William,[3] Thomas,[2] Robert[1]*), born Aug. 21, 1816; married August, 1843, Mary Newton Thomas, born Dec. 12, 1814.
Children :

66. i. JACOB THOMAS.[8] b. May 10, 1844.
ii. SAMUEL PRICE.[6] b. July 19, 1846,
iii. CATHARINE TURNER THOMAS,[8] b. May 9, 1848; d. May 19, 1852.
iv. HENRY WALTER FORTUNE,[8] b. Jan. 9, 1850.
v. JOHN THOMAS.[8] b. Nov. 26, 1851; d. June 1, 1873.
vi. ANN NEWTON THOMAS,[8] b. Feb. 10, 1855; m. Robert Blum of Easton, Pa.

66. Rev. JACOB THOMAS[8] ELWELL (*Samuel B.,[7] Samuel S.,[6] Alexander,[6] John,[4] William,[3] Thomas,[2] Robert[1]*). born at Philadelphia, Pa., May 10, 1844; married at Bassein, Burmah, May 14. 1879. Cornelia Hathaway, daughter of Stephen and Cornelia (Hathaway) Rand of Holyoke, Mass., born Oct. 22, 1842: a granddaughter of Rev. Thomas Rand, the founder and first pastor of the First Baptist Church of Holyoke (then West Springfield), Mass.

He graduated from Lewisburg, Pa., in 1871, and from Crozer Theological Seminary in 1874. After pastorates at Lincolnville and Bloomfield, Pa., he went as a missionary, under the Baptist Missionary Union, to the Bassein Mission, among the Karens in Burmah, where his widow still labors.

He returned to this country in 1882, and by a series of circumstances was prevented from returning to Burmah, as he had intended. He did good service for the cause of missions as well as for Christian work at large, however, and was laboring with intense zeal when overcome by heat at Washington, D. C., in the summer of 1888. He died at Germantown, Pa., July 16, 1888. He was widely honored and beloved, and his early death was deeply mourned.

[From the outset of his literary life, he was interested in family history; and during his last ten or twelve years he labored assiduously to solve the problems of the Elwell Genealogy. Laboring under many disadvantageous circumstances, however, he failed to embody all his extensive researches in a form which any other person could use. But he deserves lasting honor for gathering and compiling the substance of the foregoing pages. His widow has conscientiously and affectionately borne the expense of copying, verifying, completing and publishing. The Elwell family at large may be reckoned on to recompense her well for what is such a valuable contribution.—Editor.]

---

1. Robert.
- 2. Samuel.
  - 8. Samuel.
  - 9. Jacob.
    - 30. Vinson.
    - 31. William.
  - 10. Robert.
    - 32. Robert.
    - 33. Samuel.
    - 34. Benjamin.
    - 35. Joseph.
    - 36. John.
  - 11. Ebenezer.
  - 12. Thomas.
- 3. John.
  - 13. John.
    - 37. John.
    - 38. Andrew.
    - 39. Abraham.
- 4. Isaac.
  - 14. Isaac.
  - 15. Jonathan.
    - 40. Nathaniel.
    - 41. Jonathan.
    - 42. David.
    - 43. Paine.
  - 16. Eleazer.
  - 17. David.
    - 44. David.
  - 18. Joshua.
    - 45. Isaac.
    - 46. Joshua.
    - 47. Thomas.
    - 48. Mark.
    - 49. Aaron.
    - 50. William.
    - 51. Josiah.
- 5. Josiah.
  - 19. Elias.
    - 52. Elias.
    - 53. Daniel.
    - 54. Nehemiah.
  - 20. Nehemiah.
  - 21. William.
- 6. Joseph.
  - 22. Hezekiah.
  - 23. Joseph.
  - 24. Samuel.
  - 25. Benjamin.
- 7. Thomas.
  - 26. Thomas.
    - 55. Thomas.
    - 56. Josiah.
  - 27. William.
    - 57. John.
    - 58. William.
  - 28. John.
    - 59. John.
  - 29. Samuel.
    - 60. Jacob.
    - 61. Samuel.
    - 62. Abraham.

ELWELLS IN THE REVOLUTION.

FROM THE STATE OF MASSACHUSETTS.

[Copied from Archives in the office of the Secretary of State.]

Aaron, served in Azariah Alvard's company, Badlam's regt.; his name appears in a return of clothing, dated at Northfield, April 23, 1787.

Andrew, Gloucester, in Roby's co., Moses Little's regt., aged 20 yrs; enlisted May 29, 1775, served 8 months; signed order for pay Dec. 11, 1775.

Benjamin, Buxton, credited to Rowley, served 4 days at Falmouth on the day that it was set on fire by the enemy; marched to prevent the enemy from landing; roll dated at Buxton, Dec. 14, 1775. Enlisted Feb. 20, 1777, for three years, in Daniel Lane's co., Ichabod Alden's regt.; mustered by Winslow, muster master, and by a continental man, at Albany, Jan. 14, 1778. Certified at Cherry Valley Feb 24 1778, and May 4, 1779; also in Holden's co., Brook's regt., from Jan. 1, 1780, to Feb. 13, 1780.

Caleb, Cape Ann, in John Row's co. of Ebenezer Bridge's regt, (27th) from May 29 to Nov. 9, 1775; papers dated at Cambridge.

David, Gloucester, corporal, in Enoch Putnam's co., John Mansfield's (19th,) regt., in the 8 months service; enlisted May 18, 1775; order for bounty coat, dated at Winter Hill, Oct. 27, 1775.

David, Gloucester, corporal, enlisted May 22, 1775, in Barnabas Dodge's co., Gerrish's (Baldwin's.) regt.; re-enlisted in the new establishment army Nov. 24, 1775; enlisted for 1 year, Dec. 31, 1775.; was in camp at New York July 18, 1776; served to Dec. 31, 1776, when he re-enlisted for 6 weeks at Trenton. Returned his gun at Chatham Feb. 12, 1777.

Elias, Gloucester, enlisted June 6, 1775, in Joseph Roby's co., Moses Little's regt. in the 8 months service; æ. 20 years; gave order for bounty coat Dec. 11, 1775.

Elias, Gloucester, enlisted in Daniel Warren's co. July 19, and served to Dec. 31, 1775, in coast defence at Gloucester. Enlisted Jan. 16, and served to Feb. 29, 1776.

Elias Jr. (perhaps the same as the foregoing.) Gloucester, enlisted March 1, 1776 in Daniel Warner's regt., and served in coast defence at Gloucester till Aug. 31, 1776.

Henry Butler, on petition of Jedediah Preble, in behalf of several persons of Falmouth, Casco Bay, dated at Boston, Aug. 13, 1781, the Council advised that a commission be issued to him as commander of the Brigantine "Union," a privateer, mounting 10 carriage guns, burthen, 100 tons, navigated by 18 men, with 200 wt. of powder, and shot in proportion.

Jabez, reported in official list of men belonging to Hadley, Amherst and Belchertown, in Col. Ruggles Woodbridge's regt.; dated Cambridge April 25, 1775. Capt. Thomas Waite Foster's train of artillery.

Jabez, Hardwick, was reported Feb. 25, 1778, as enlisted in Warren's co. of Alden's regt. (4th Worcester.) for 3 years.

Jesse, enlisted July 1, 1780, in Joseph Browning's co. of Seth Murray's regt. (Hampshire co.) raised for 3 months, by resolve, June 22, 1780, to reinforce the Continental Army: served 3 months, 4 days.

John, claimed by Buxton, allowed to Rowley, in Daniel Lamb's co. of Alden's regt., mustered at Albany Jan. 14, 1778, by Winslow, m.m. and by a continental m.m.

John, Hadley, 24 years old, 5 feet 9 inches high, of light complexion, arrived at Springfield July 6, 1780, under command of Capt. Dix, in 7th division; enlisted for 6 months to reinforce the Continental Army.

John, Gloucester, reported in the crew of the ship America; was 22 years old, 6 feet high.

Simeon signs an order for advance pay on account of service in Eliakim Smith's co. Jonathan Ward's regt. at Cambridge, June 8, 1775.

Solomon, Gloucester, reported in Putnam's co., 19th regt., Oct. 6, 1775.

Thomas, sergeant in Jonathan Wales' co. in the regt. commanded by Lt. Col. S. Williams, engaged Dec. 20, 1776, discharged March 23, 1777.

William, Gloucester, 14 years of age, 4 feet, 6 inches high, was in the crew of the ship America, June 8, 1780.

William, in 8 months service, in Barnabas Dodge's co. of Loammi Baldwin's regt.; wages paid at Chelsea for the month of August, 1775; had a furlough for 4 days in Sept. 1775; signed order for bounty coat Dec. 27, 1775.

INDEX TO ELWELLS.

Acton, 9.
Benson, 9.
Farnes, 8, 13.
Lassett, 9.
Bennett, 6.
Berryman, 21.
Bishop, 12.
Blum, 22.
Brick, 17.
Brown, Browne, 4, 12, 14, 18.
Cary, 13.
Cheeseman, 12.
Choate, 9.
Clambole, Clembole, 15.
Clifford, 7.
Collins, 4, 8, 14.
Cook, 8.
Corney, 18.
Crane, 16.
Davis, 8.
Day, 14.
Dehber, 5.
Depping, 14.
Derby, 4.
Dolliver, Dolliber, 5, 7, 14.
Dudbridge, 4.
Duriel, 12.
Dutch, 7, 9.
Edgecomb, 12, 13.
Ellery, 15.
Emerson, 6, 7, 12.
Fennicke, Fenwick, 15.
Foard, 10.
Gardner, 7, 12.
Garrison, 16.
Gaylor, 3.
Gearing, 18.
Gerrett, 16.
Giddings, 18.
Glover, 3.
Grenaway, Greenway, 3, 8.
Grover, 15, 20.
Hadley, 15.
Hall, 11.
Hathaway, 22.
Hibbard, 19.
Hill, 4, 13.
Hodges, 10.
Hodgskins, 7.
Holland, 3, 4.
Hollingsworth, 7.
Holton, 16, 17.
Howes, 21.
Hull, 13.
Hutchings, 17.
Johnson, 12.
Joslyn, 13.
Kibbe, 4.
Killingsworth, 16.
Lamb, 19.
Lamer, 20.
Leach, 6.
Lock, 16.

Low, Lowe, 14.
Ludlow, 3.
Lurvey, 17.
Manning, 9.
Mariner, 14.
Mather, 3.
Mecham, 7.
Millett, 8, 20.
Milward, 4.
Moody, 19.
Moore, More, 15, 21.
Newman, 16, 17.
Nickolds, 10.
Ober, 13.
Paine, 14.
Parsons, 6.
Paullin, 12, 20.
Pierce, Pearce, 14, 19.
Piles, 10.
Pinson, 7.
Pope, 1, 22, 24, 30.
Priest, 3.
Prince, 8.
Rand, 22.
Ray, 17.
Reed, 12.
Richards, 3.
Riggs, 14.
Robinson, 13, 18.
Rocket, 3.
Row, Rowe, 6, 8.
Ruderford, 17.
Rytland, 13.
Sallows, Sallowes, Swallows, 13, 14.
Sampson, 7.
Sawtelle, 20.
Shourds, 11.
Smith, 7, 18.
Stanwood, 19, 20.
Stevens, 8, 12, 18.
Stover, 8.
Stratton, Stretton, 4, 19.
Tarr, 7.
Thomas, 22.
Tucker, 8.
Turner, 9.
Tuttle, 4.
Urin, 8.
Vanmeter, 16.
Vinson, 12, 17.
Wallace, 12.
Wallis, 18.
Walling, 10.
Warner, 8.
Way, 3, 4.
Weeks, 15.
Wheeler, 14.
White, 10, 11, 15.
Wilkeins, 3.
Wilkinson, 4.
Williams, 15.
Wonuarton, 4.
York, 19, 20.

A CALL FOR MATERIAL FOR A COMPLETE ELWELL GENEALOGY.

MANY persons ask for it and are disappointed that there is none to be found. Hundreds will welcome this first part of such a work; but they want a book giving names and sketches of Elwells and the children of Elwell mothers now or recently living in America; with pictures of persons and places here and in England, and all that makes a first-class, up-to-date family history. The practical question is: *Will you have it!*

Now there must first be a gathering of hundreds of local, family stories; then a critical scrutiny of these reports and an arrangement of them into their branches and clusters; and this requires the search of a score or more of town, county and state records and archives, to get from public authorities such official statements as will make the genealogy entirely trustworthy in all its combinations. Who will do this, and what will feed and clothe the compiler, pay postage and stationery bills and fees and expenses ?

Will you answer this question !

To begin with: the subscriber will consent to receive and tabulate all properly prepared family records and narratives which you Elwells who read this will send to him. He will make investigations as well and as far as you will contribute the means; and will hold all material you thus contribute and enable him to prepare, ready for the making of an Elwell Genealogy when it is practicable.

Already he has a most important clue to the English home of Robert and Joane Elwell, which he will follow out to definite information if volunteers will furnish the means; and his experience and reputation furnish a guarantee, he believes, that his methods of work will be thorough, economical and faithful to the truth.

A model for reports is given on the following pages; substitute for the whimsical fancies which are woven into the story of the (imaginary) Mannett family, a story as full of details concerning your own immediate family. *Guess at nothing; investigate and have proof of every figure and circumstance you relate.*

Keep a copy of what you send; state your authority for your statements; as, for instance, "taken from A. B. C.'s family Bible," or "from obituary notice," or "from gravestone." Write things you know familiarly for the benefit of readers distant in place and time.

Address, with stamp for reply,

REV. CHARLES H. POPE,

221 Columbus Ave., Boston, Mass.

MODEL FOR THE REPORT OF A FAMILY TO A GENEALOGIST.

Published by Charles Henry Pope, 221 Columbus Avenue, Boston, Mass.

1. John Mannett, son of Jacob and Susan (Ballard) Mannett, grandson of Adam and Ruth (Brown) Mannett, of Dover, N. H., born at Albion, N. H., Oct. 3, 1795; learned the trade of tailor. He enlisted, April 1, 1813, in the 3d Continental regt. of N. Y., Col. Otis Gray, and served 8 months; received a pension from 1829 till his death. He spent his youth at Albion, but removed about 1815 to Troy, N. Y., where he was two years a clerk and then a partner in the house of Van der Velde and Work, provision dealers. He was a member of the Baptist church, a trustee of Albion Academy, an ardent Whig. He married at Dort, Vt., May 1, 1823, Mary, dau. of Hugh and Jane (Anderson) McNutt, born Nov. 5, 1801, at Dort: her parents were natives of Paisley, Scotland; she died of pneumonia Oct. 30, 1830. Mr. Mannett married second, in Troy, N. Y., Aug. 1, 1838, Julia Ann, daughter of Dr. Arthur and Maria (Hill) Chase, born at Atkinson, N. H., Jan. 3, 1809; her father was an eminent physician and the author of several medical works; she was a teacher in the public schools of Boston, Mass., for six years previous to her marriage. She died of typhoid fever March 2, 1874. Mr. Mannett died of gastritis July 4, 1881, in the house where he had lived more than fifty years, and where all his children were born.

Children:

i. Abram Mannett, b. March 16, 1824; d. of measles Sept. 13, 1832.

ii. Laura Mannett, b. March 3, 1826; married May 3, 1845, George Hay Bell, Jr., of Orange, Vt., where they reside. Children: (1) Willie Bell, b. May 14, 1847; (2) Arthur Bell, b. July 3, 1849; (3) Ora Bailey Bell, b. Oct. 8, 1857: (4) George Hay Bell, Jr., b. Jan. 1, 1868, grad. Dartmouth College 1892, Harvard Law School 1895, and is an attorney in Alta Pinta, Porto Rico. Mrs. Bell is a member of the Daughters of the Revolution.

2. iii. Hugh McNutt Mannett, b. Oct. 1, 1829.

iv. Mary Anderson Mannett, b. Nov. 3, 1839; m. in Troy, N. Y., April 1, 1863, Leonard Dow, of Troy, then captain of co. K, 75th N. Y. Vol. Infantry; he was promoted to the rank of Major for bravery shown at the battle of Bland, but died at Annapolis Dec. 3, 1863, of wounds received in that battle. Child: Hope Murray Dow, b. at Washington, D. C., June 3, 1864; is a clerk in the Treasury department at Washington. Mrs. Dow married second, Feb. 16, 1873, James Elson Farr, M.D., of Fairfax, Va.; they have one child, Thomas Farr, b. May 2, 1879, a student in the Manual Training School of Troy, N. Y., in the class of 1900.

v. Mark Mannett, b. April 1, 1850; was educated in the public schools of Troy, graduating from the High School at the age of sixteen. Travelled in the U. S. four years as a salesman for the Wild Sewing Machine Co.; spent three and a half years in European travel. Entered the firm of which his father had so long been a member in 1880, and still continues in it. Representative to the State Assembly, 1883, 1886; chairman of the State Valuation Commission, 1890-1; member of several fraternal organizations, of the N. E. Historic-Genealogical Society, and an officer in the N. Y. Society for the Prevention of Cruelty to Women. Not married.

vi. OLIVER MANNETT, *b.* Aug. 30, 1852; learned the trade of tailor and carries on the business at Buffalo, N. Y. Not married.

2. HUGH McNUTT MANNETT *(John, Jacob, Adam)*, *b.* at Troy, N. Y., Oct. 1, 1829; graduated from the Polytechnic Institute in the class of 1841; spent four years in the employ of the Oldtown Locomotive Works, of which he became superintendent in 1845. He resigned April 16, 1861, to accept the position of brigade commissary on the staff of Gen. Alvan Quick of Vermont. Was transferred by order of Secretary Stanton to the department of Construction and Repair, with the rank of colonel, and had charge of the Washington and Annapolis Railroad, which had been taken into military possession. He was mustered out of service for disability Aug. 15, 1864, and resumed the post which he had left three years before. Has declined to accept a pension. Is president of the First National Bank of Oldtown; one of the regents of the Smithsonian Institution, at Washington, D. C.; a trustee of Yale College; an elder in the Presbyterian church. *He married* at Utica, Aug. 3, 1872, Lucy Nimro, *daughter of* Capt. Thayer *and* Alice May (Stokes) Quinsey, *of Boston*, Mass., *b.* in Bombay, India, on board her father's ship, the Gallant, Aug. 3, 1854.

Children:

i. EDMOND QUINSEY MANNETT, *b.* June 1, 1873; grad. Annapolis Naval Academy in 1897; an ensign in U. S. Navy; member N. Y. Society of Colonial Wars.

ii. ALICE THAYER MANNETT, *b.* Sept. 18, 1874; grad. Smith College in 1898; teacher of History at Lone Star Academy, N. M.

3. iii. STANTON MANNETT, *b.* June 10, 1875.

iv. THOMAS BREED MANNETT, *b.* Oct. 22, 1876; junior partner in the firm of Van der Velde and Work, Troy, N. Y.

v. WAIT CLAP MANNETT, *b.* July 4, 1890.

vi. BENJAMIN MANNETT, *b.* Dec. 31, 1897.

N.B.—Every name must be written out in full: *e. g.*, not E. Q. but Edmond Quinsey. All dates must be complete; not 1897, but Dec. 31, 1897. All married women's maiden names must be given: not Maria Chase, but Maria (Hill) Chase. Follow the style of the foregoing " model," and make as full a record of real persons. Tell the authority or source of information for your statements.